The
Star Maiden

An Ojibway Tale

Retold by

Barbara Juster Esbensen

Illustrated by

Helen K. Davie

Little, Brown and Company
Boston Toronto London

Also by Barbara Juster Esbensen and Helen K. Davie:

Ladder to the Sky

Author's Note

In their own language, the Ojibway, or Chippewa people, are known as
Anishinabe—"original people." Because their culture and language are based on
stories told, not written down, there are often different versions of the same tale.
The one I am telling here is based on the 1850 work by the Ojibway chief
Kah-ge-ga-gah-bowh, who later took the name George Copway. In 1850 he wrote
a book setting down Ojibway history, customs, and legends because he was
afraid this valuable information would one day disappear entirely.

— *B.J.E.*

First Edition

The Star Maiden is a retelling of "The Star and the Lily"
from *The Traditional History and Characteristic Sketches of
the Ojibway Nation*
by George Copway, Chief of the Ojibway Nation
(London: Charles Gilpin, Publishers, 1850).

Library of Congress Cataloging-in-Publication Data
Esbensen, Barbara Juster.
  The star maiden.
  ISBN 0-316-24951-3 (hc)
  ISBN 0-316-24955-6 (pb)
    1. Chippewa Indians—Legends. 2. Indians of North
America—Legends. I. Davie, Helen. II. Title.
E99.C6E72 1988   398.2'6'08997   87-3247

        HC: 10 9 8 7 6 5 4
        PB: 10 9 8 7 6 5 4 3 2

            WOR

Designed by Trisha Hanlon

*Published simultaneously in Canada
by Little, Brown & Company (Canada) Limited*

Printed in the United States of America

Once there was a time,
long, long ago,
when all the tribes in the land
lived in peace.

There were no wars among them.
Summer was always in the air.
The streams were clear and pure,
and filled with fish.

Bird-song rang from every tree
and the earth was rich
with everything the people needed.

All day long, they hunted
and fished. They gathered fruits
and nuts. They made birchbark canoes
to carry them lightly
along rivers and across the wide lakes.

But at night, when work was done,
the people loved to watch the sky.
They loved to see the silver disk
of the moon climb the darkness.
They loved to watch the stars
flicker their icy fire.

One night
when the sky above the prairie
was glittering with starlight,
they saw something new.

It was the brightest star
anyone had ever seen.
As they watched, it began to move.
It fell almost to earth!

Then it stopped. They could see it
hanging like a white blaze
near the top of a faraway hill.
What could this mean? They wondered
and they watched night after night.

It never moved from the hilltop.
Days went by.
At last the great chief spoke.
"Let some braves go into the far hills.
Let them see this thing
and let them tell us what it is!"

So the braves went into the far hills.
When they came back they said,
"We saw something shining there.
It hung in the top of a dark pine tree.
It did not answer us.
It made us feel afraid!"

That very night,
one of those young braves
had a dream. A silver maiden
came into his dream.
She shone with silver light.
She spoke to him. Her voice was like
a thread of silver.

She held out her shining arms to him
"I am tired of wandering across the sky," she said.
"Your world calls to me.

"I love the blowing winds
I love the colors I see below me.
I love your rivers and lakes.
I want to dip my hands
in the clear water
that shines up at me.

"I have watched your people.
I have watched the children playing
in the villages and tumbling
in the prairie grass.

"I want to live among you.
No more will I wander in the dark sky.
Let your wisest people help me.
Let them tell me what form I will take.
Then I can live on your land forever."

The young brave woke up.
It was still night.
His dream was gone.
The silver maiden had vanished, too.

When he looked at the far-off hills
he saw the shining light hanging
in the top of the dark pine tree.
Then he fell asleep again.

In the morning,
the young brave told the chief
about his strange dream.
The chief called the wisest men and women together.
They sat in their council circle
and listened.

The chief stood up. He spoke.

"A star wants to live on earth," he said.
"Our people will welcome her.
The blue air over the prairie
will fill with bird-song
to honor her coming.

"On earth, she cannot be a shining star
So, let her choose the form she will take.

"She can be a flower growing in the earth.
She can be a fish swimming in the water.
She can be a bird soaring in the clear air.
Her home will be where she finds
a peaceful resting-place.
Go! You must find her and tell her this!"

The chief and the wise ones
stood up and slowly walked around their fire.
They sang a song of welcome
and threw sweet wood on the flames.
The fragrant smoke rose up, up
into the morning sky.
It was a greeting to the star.

The next night, the young brave left the village.
He went into the faraway hills
where silver light hung
in the top of a tree.
He looked up, and the light floated
down to where he stood.
It was the silver maiden of his
dream. He turned, and she followed.

She drifted above him,
lighting his way through the darkness.

When the young brave came home
the people crept out to see the star maiden.
Her soft light hung in the air
over their wigwams all night long.

Morning came, and the star maiden slipped into
the center of a rose that grew on a hillside.
The people heard her voice in the air above them.
"This shall be my home. In this flower
I shall live on earth."

But the next day they heard her voice again.
"This rose is too far from the village," she said.
"I never see the people I love."
So she left the rose and floated down
to the wide grassy prairie.

Flowers of every color grew there.
"I shall live on this prairie,"
the star maiden said to the wind.
She chose a small flower
as blue as the sky.
"This is where I will stay."

But something was wrong.
Every day the earth shook
and trembled under her.
Herds of great buffalo trampled
the ground. Their hoofs dug at the earth.

"I cannot rest here!" she cried out.
And that night, the people saw her shining light
rise into the dark sky above their heads.

They were sad.
They were afraid she would leave forever.
Their earth did not welcome her after all.
She could not find a peaceful home.

The star maiden drifted over the lake.
She hung there. Her reflection
floated on the dark water.
Floating on the water were the reflections
of all her sky-sisters, too.

The people watched.
Then they heard her silver voice again.
"Sisters, sisters," she called.
"Stop your wandering! Find rest with me.
These quiet waters
will be our home. Come!"

The people saw the sky shake
with glittering points of light.
They saw the dark lake come alive
with stars.

"What does this mean?" they asked.
The wise ones smiled. The chief smiled, too.
"Let us go to our beds and sleep now," he said.
"Our star maiden has found a home at last."

The night wind blew. Loons called. Owls hooted.
When morning came, something was different.

Hundreds of stars were floating
on the blue lake.
NO! Not stars!
Hundreds of starflowers floated there!
Water lilies!

The star maiden had found her place on earth.
Her star-sisters had listened.
They had stopped wandering
across the night sky, too.
They had dropped into the lake
to join the star maiden in her new home.
All the people floated out in their canoes.
They leaned over to touch the creamy petals.

Water lilies!
They are stars that fell from the deep sky
one night long, long ago.

If you see them, touch them gently.
Their petals shine in the sun
like the stars that lived and sparkled
in the sky once upon a time.

Water lilies! Touch them gently
and remember.